Rabbit & Possum

Dana Wulfekotte

Greenwillow Books
An Imprint of HarperCollinsPublishers

Rabbit & Possum
Copyright © 2018 by Dana Wulfekotte
All rights reserved. Manufactured in China. For information address
HarperCollins Children's Books, a division of HarperCollins Publishers,
195 Broadway, New York, NY 10007.
www.harpercollinschildrens.com

The art was done with pencil on paper and digitally colored in Photoshop.
The text type is Palatino.

Library of Congress Cataloging-in-Publication Data is available.
ISBN 978-0-06-245581-9 (hardback)

18 19 20 21 22 SCP 10 9 8 7 6 5 4 3 2 1
First Edition

Greenwillow Books

For Sean

Rabbit had spent all morning
getting her burrow ready.
Possum was coming over!
Rabbit had swept away the dust bunnies
and prepared their favorite snacks.

Psst...

But now Possum
was fast asleep.

No matter what Rabbit did . . .

Possum didn't stir

until there was a rustling in the bushes.

Off Possum sprinted, down the hill
and up a very tall tree.
Rabbit raced after him.

Rabbit tried to follow Possum.
But as it turns out . . .

rabbits aren't very good at climbing trees.

Rabbit wanted to help Possum get down,

but all her ideas made him a little uneasy.

Rabbit needed a better plan.

There was,
however,

one more problem.

The ladder was too short.

Possum was not feeling very optimistic.

But Rabbit refused to give up.
She had one more idea.

In a flash, Rabbit took off into the woods.
All Possum could do was wait.

So he waited.

And waited.

And waited.

Finally, Rabbit zipped
back to the tree.

Moose followed at his own pace.

I don't like
to be rushed.

Possum was sure this was Rabbit's worst idea yet.

Possum stared at Moose's giant antlers.
And his flaring nostrils.
And his enormous mouth.

Possum took a deep breath.

Soon enough, Possum was back on the ground.

Rabbit had been right.
Moose wasn't a monster, after all.

This was, by far, Rabbit's best idea.